THE MEG & ROB'S WITCH TRICKS COLLECTION:

Book 1	Book 2
The Wicked Stew	No Win With A Twin

Books are available on Amazon.com

Meg & Rob's Witch Tricks

Book 1

The Wicked Stew

Meg picks up the heavy spell book and faces raven Rob. "We are going to conjure ourselves a servant goblin. Servant goblins are strong and very useful; they handle chores, do laundry, dishes and even clean up stoves," says Meg.

Meg carefully opens the thick, dusty spell book cover, which had been forgotten in the attic for ages. Flipping through the stiff pages she suddenly shouts, "Ah-ha! Look here on page thirteen... the instructions!"

Rob reads the long list of instructions, and realizing the task at hand, starts picking his feathers anxiously. "Making the goblin is a chore in itself, not a simple task, even for an older magician," he thinks grimly.

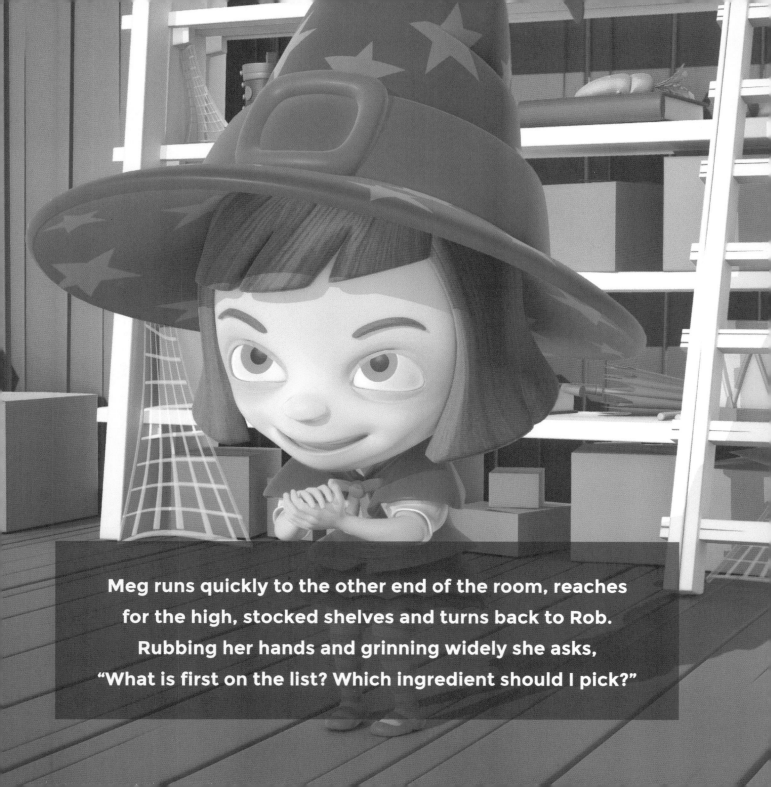

Meg runs quickly to the other end of the room, reaches
for the high, stocked shelves and turns back to Rob.
Rubbing her hands and grinning widely she asks,
"What is first on the list? Which ingredient should I pick?"

The list is long and very specific. A servant goblin needs a tough and sturdy torso to handle his chores. Rob gulps, plucks up his courage and shouts to Meg, "First ingredient on the list, bones! At least eight!"

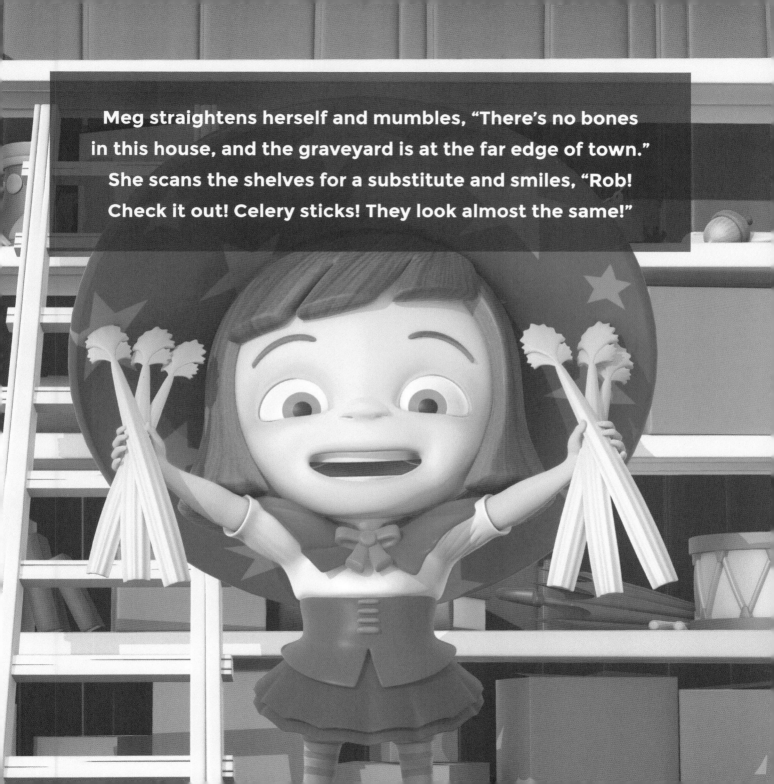

Meg straightens herself and mumbles, "There's no bones in this house, and the graveyard is at the far edge of town." She scans the shelves for a substitute and smiles, "Rob! Check it out! Celery sticks! They look almost the same!"

Meg tosses the celery into the cauldron, and pleased with herself, she turns back to Rob and asks, "What is next on the list? Number two." Rob flies above her and crows, "Impossible! It says here that we need a skull!"

"What is the head size that best fits a goblin?" Meg asks herself with puzzlement, not willing to give up yet. There must be an object inside the house that equals the required length and mass.

Rob settles down and thinks. "I know," he says and flies out swiftly to the garden. Stepping in, after a few moments, he rolls in a heavy, round cabbage. "Perfect," Meg says, and turns back to the book.

"Next on the list is an ugly nose from a troll: lumpy, thick and covered with moles." Meg looks at it puzzled. Suddenly smirking, she skips to a big box in the corner, tilts it and tries to reach inside.

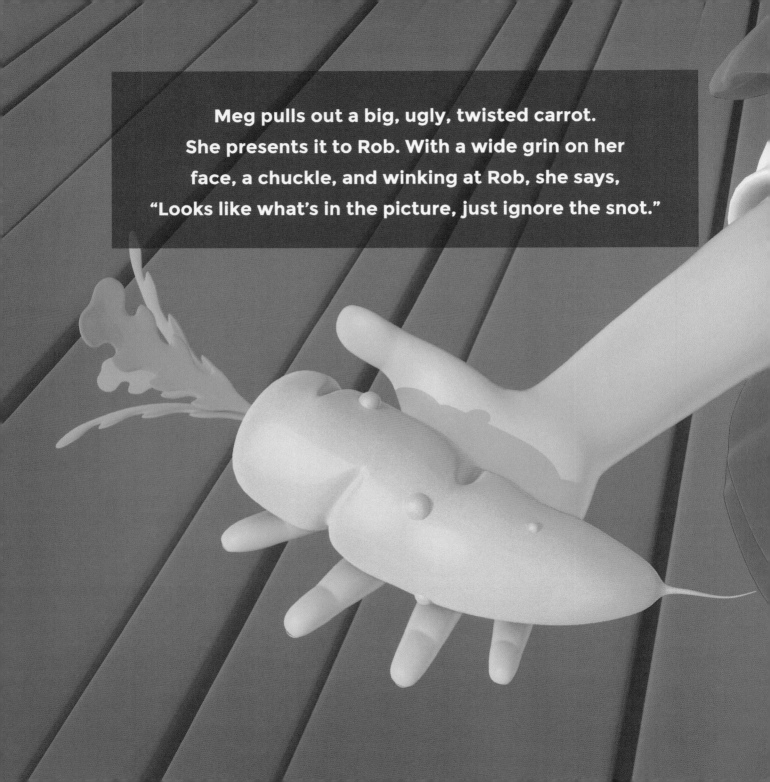

Meg pulls out a big, ugly, twisted carrot.
She presents it to Rob. With a wide grin on her
face, a chuckle, and winking at Rob, she says,
"Looks like what's in the picture, just ignore the snot."

Rob tilts his head, nods and says, "Might as well."
He flies back to the book, to read what is next.
After a moment, Rob suddenly recoils and shrieks,
"What? A lump of white hair from a unicorn's tail?"

"No, way!" Meg answers, thinking it's cruel. "A hairless unicorn, even just missing his tail, won't be able to go out or play. We will find something else," she concludes, approaching the shelves determinedly.

Meg tosses boxes all over the place and turns cans upside down, looking for another solution. Finally, she presents Rob with a stack of spaghetti. "There, nobody will notice the difference. Done!"

Meg leans forward, scatters the spaghetti bundle over the pot and starts stirring the thick mix with glowing eyes. "We are close, I can feel it. Quickly, which item is next?" Meg sighs, wiping her brow with excitement.

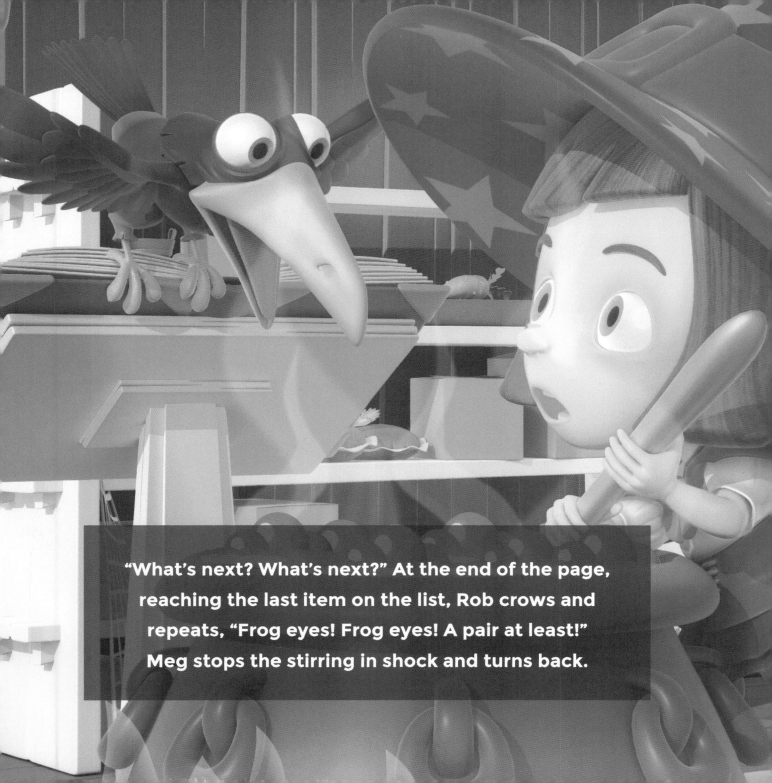

"What's next? What's next?" At the end of the page, reaching the last item on the list, Rob crows and repeats, "Frog eyes! Frog eyes! A pair at least!" Meg stops the stirring in shock and turns back.

Frogs are all over and easy to find this season.
But Meg doesn't like that, it just grosses her out.
She climbs up the ladder and reaches for a tiny can
on the top shelf. After a moment, Meg jumps down
with two olives in her hand.

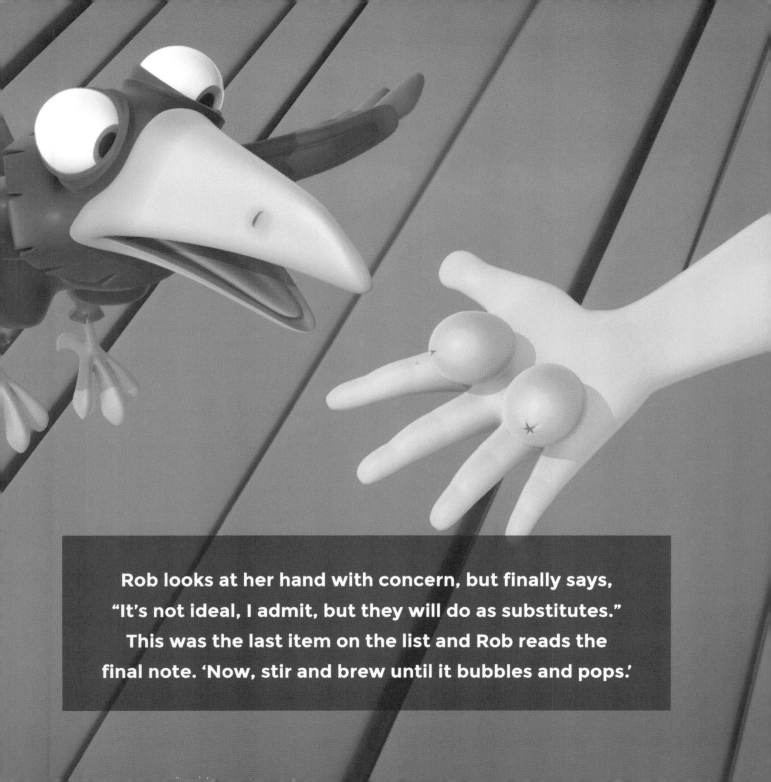

Rob looks at her hand with concern, but finally says, "It's not ideal, I admit, but they will do as substitutes." This was the last item on the list and Rob reads the final note. 'Now, stir and brew until it bubbles and pops.'

Meg keeps stirring anxiously. Rob looks into the cauldron, tapping his foot. Conjuring the goblin took almost all day. The pot is boiling, but nothing moves inside and Meg says, "What went wrong? I don't get it. Where is the goblin?"

Meg takes a small spoon to taste a sample and check. After a long pause her eyes brighten and she looks at Rob, "No goblin, it's a pity. But grab some bowls from the sink. We just cooked ourselves a wicked stew, spicy and thick!"

THANK YOU!

If you enjoyed this book, please consider taking a minute to write an honest review on Amazon. Reviews are the lifeblood of indie authors and your contribution would be greatly appreciated.

Best regards,
Daniel & April

APRIL PETER

April is a prolific illustrator and cartoonist turned children's books writer. In 2017 she converted her successful animated short "Ann Can't Sleep" and self-published it as an illustrated Kindle and paperback bedtime story for preschoolers.

DANIEL SHNEOR

Daniel is an expert 3D animation artist, teacher, and a children's book writer and illustrator. After publishing several animated mobile app stories (including his series featuring Koto the Samurai Guard Dog), he turned to self-publishing on Amazon.

MORE BOOKS BY THE AUTHORS:

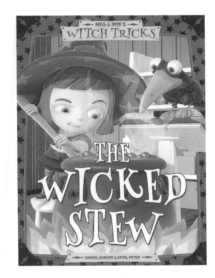

Book 1
The Wicked Stew

Book 2
No Win With
A Twin

Ann Can't
Sleep

Books are available on Amazon.com

NEWS & UPDATES

For special insider access to future releases,
promotions and more, please follow the
link below and subscribe to our newsletter.

www.light-sleepers.com/subscribe

Printed in Great Britain
by Amazon

78500046R00020